This book belongs to:

How Mitzvah Giraffe Got His Long, Long Neck

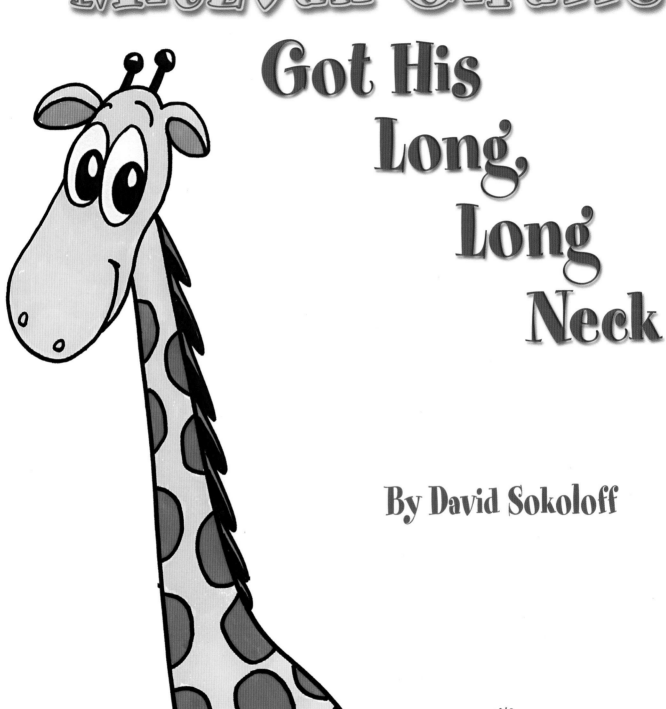

By David Sokoloff

The Judaica Press, Inc.

For Tuvia

ISBN 0-910818-20-7

Edited by: Nachum Shapiro
Page layout & typography by: Zisi Berkowitz

The Judaica Press, Inc.
718-972-6200   800-972-6201
info@judaicapress.com
www.judaicapress.com

Manufactured in Hong Kong

Let me tell you a story. Please try not to laugh.
This story's about a short-necked giraffe.
He lived long ago, in a land far away,
in a place where the sun shone brightly each day.
But despite the beautiful hills, trees and sun,
this little giraffe never had any fun.

This giraffe, called Mopey, was always so sad.
He never felt happy, just gloomy and bad.

He would kvetch and moan and always complain:
"My knees are aching. I'm sure it will rain.
I've got such a headache. My nose is all runny.
My feet are sore, and my tongue feels funny…"

One day, as he kvetched about all his bad luck,
he was stopped in his tracks by old Mrs. Duck.

She said, "Why are you always in such a bad mood?
You can't go around being kvetchy and rude.
Go to the forest and see the old goat.
He gives good advice, so be sure to take notes!"

Mopey Giraffe just grumbled and groaned,
but he went to the goat, and sat down with a moan.
The goat welcomed him. He gave him a seat
and said, "Poor giraffe, you look tired and beat."

"Oh," Mopey sighed, "my life is just rotten.
I ask for help, but I'm always forgotten.
Nobody listens, even though I complain
day after day about all of my pain."

"I cry to my friends almost every day,
but rather than listen they just run away."

The wise old goat listened and nodded his head.
"Well, I have a suggestion for you," he said.

"Instead of worrying about the aches in your bones,
instead of the kvetching and sighing and moans,
go look for ways to gladden your buddies.
Lend them your hanky, help with their studies,
bake them some cupcakes or knit them a sweater.
If you try to help others, you too will feel better."

"I don't know," whined Mopey.

"It sounds kind of weird."

"Just try," said the goat, as he stroked his grey beard.

As he left, Mopey thought,
"I don't understand!
Will I feel so much better
just by lending a hand?"

All of a sudden,
he smelled and saw smoke!
"That tree is on fire!" he yelled.
"It's no joke!"

He ran to the tree, as close as he dared,
And saw three baby birds in their nest, really scared!

"Help, help!" cried the birds.
"Our mother's not here!
And the fire is getting
so frightfully near!"

Mopey realized this was no time to kvetch.

"To get to those birds, I must stretch, stretch,

S T R E T C H ! "

16

"Don't be scared," he called out
as the fire quickly rose.
"Just jump from your nest
right onto my nose!"

"Now down my long neck
you can all safely slide.
Just think of it as
an amusement park ride!"

The baby birds knew
they must not fool around.
So they slid down his neck
and plopped to the ground.

WHee!

When the baby birds' mother
returned before long,
she was so very grateful
she sang him a song:

"Oh, thank you, Giraffe!
Thanks again and again!
You're a wonderful hero!
A fabulous friend!"

"Mitzvah Giraffe
will be your new name!
We're so proud to know you!"

21

Said Mitzvah Giraffe,
"I finally feel good!
Just like the wise old goat
said that I would!"

So our story has come
to a wonderful end.
Mitzvah Giraffe
became
everyone's friend!

Now when you see giraffes in a book or the zoo,

let it serve as a friendly reminder to you.

Be like Mitzvah Giraffe and do kind things for others,

and be happy while helping your sisters and brothers.

There may be some Mitzvah Giraffe inside you.

So stretch to the limits, and you will grow, too!